POWER

POWER

Adapted for
BearManor Media
by Philip Proctor

BearManor Media

2017

Power

For information, address:

BearManor Media
P. O. Box 71426
Albany, GA 31708

bearmanormedia.com

Typesetting and layout by John Teehan

Published in the USA by BearManor Media

ISBN—978-1-62933-181-2

I dedicate this work
to my dear departed partner,
Peter Bergman:
the real power behind POWER.

Table of Contents

A Foreword, Into the Past

IN THE SUMMER OF 1990, Nation Public Radio broadcast live from New York, the nightly, two-hour program, "Heat--With John Hockenberry," devoted to the arts, politics, and culture.

I was a producer on the show, and wished to honor Heat's mandate to create art, not just talk about it. One day, I spotted a post-it with Phil Proctor's telephone number stuck to the wall of "program ideas." As a long time fan of Firesign Theater, I called Philip and asked him if he wanted to contribute some comedy. He, in turn, invited Peter Bergman to join him. Philip and Peter had been friends for three decades since their days at Yale and before they teamed up with David Ossman and Phil Austin to create Firesign Theater. Proctor and Bergman also enjoyed a long run as a comedy due. However, in 1990, Firesign Theater was dormant and Proctor & Bergman had not worked together for several years.

The time was ripe for a new project. They offered to write a perform a weekly, five-minute episodic dramatic comedy series called "Power." Its premise was to lampoon the excesses of Hollywood in the late 1980's, a town that Philip Proctor proclaims as "the only place where you can get stabbed in the front."

Philip and Peter voice recorded each week's installment in Los Angeles and shipped it to New York, where I hastily added sound effects and mixed it for broadcast.

For the three of us, it was the beginning for a wonderful working relationship and deep friendship that continues today. I am forever grateful to them for putting faith in me, as they never asked to hear any of my work before agreeing to do this series.

As Power so brilliantly reveals, Proctor & Bergman are true comedy frontiersmen offering hilarious insights that often foreshadow actual events.

With them, life does follow art.

– Ted Bonnitt
December, 1998

POWER

Created by & Starring
Phil Proctor &
Peter Bergman

Co-Starring
Melinda Peterson

Featuring
Patricia Stallone

With Kristin Campbell

Produced by Ted Bonnitt
and Seventh Planet Productions

First Aired in Serial Form the Summer
of 1990 on NPR's Award-Winning "Heat"

Hosted by John Hockenberry

POWER #1: DINNER WITH PAUL

ANN: Now—life on the edge in LA.—Peter Bergman and Phil Proctor star in "Power."

SFX: RESTAURANT AMBIANCE, A TELEPHONE RINGS AND IS PICKED UP.

JOCELYN: Hello, Baldy's Le Dome. Oh, hello, Mr. Trump, what will it be? Eight at six? Oh—six at eight. Let me check. Hmmmm. I'm sorry, Mr. Trump, we're booked through Christmas, how about next year? No, Don, the restaurant is not for sale, *ciao*.

SFX: PHONE HANG UP

GEORGE: (comes on) Hello, Jocelyn.

PAUL: Jojo!

JOCELYN: Mr. Power, Mr. Scoff, right this way, gentlemen.

GEORGE: Thank you.

PAUL: Brucie…

GEORGE: Brucie! Sixty million over budget? Somebody's "Dying Harder," eh?

PAUL: Dustin, get your head out of the soup, this isn't a movie, buddy…

GEORGE: Marlon… (Brando is sobbing) Gosh, how are you?

PAUL: Oh, my. Say, Marlon, you need anything, just call my machine…

GEORGE: Good luck.

PAUL: What a shame, really.

GEORGE: I know. Thanks, Jojo. So, Paulie, how're things at the office?

PAUL: Excellent. I just packaged Nicholson and Willis in their first feature together.

GEORGE: Wow! What's it about?

PAUL: Well, it's a back-end deal. I won't know 'til the picture's finished.

GEORGE: How's the family?

PAUL: It's going into turnaround, and Astrid wants custody of the child.

GEORGE: Astrid wants Solly?

PAUL: No, no, George, Solly's out of Margo, my second wife.

GEORGE: Oh, that's right.

PAUL: Astrid wants custody of my inner child—the child within.

GEORGE: (laughs) That's new.

PAUL: Yeah. George, that's why I want you to represent me.

GEORGE: Well—actually, Paul, we've been so busy at the firm, I don't have time to practice law.

PAUL: George, this is Paul, huh? I know you're the best criminal divorce lawyer in this Zip. Now, c'mon, buddy—how much do you get?

GEORGE: I get ten thousand an hour.

PAUL: That's fair.

GEORGE: But, Paul, you're my friend and the IRS isn't. (laughs)

PAUL: Tell me.

GEORGE: So, let's barter, huh?

PAUL: Hey, I'm listening.

GEORGE: Okay, all right. You know my wife, Marcie?

PAUL: Yeah, she was my first wife.

GEORGE: Oh, yeah.

PAUL: Hey, c'mon!

GEORGE: I forgot, right? Okay? Well, she's been bitten by the acting bug—again, huh? So, I'll handle your divorce and you get Marcie the lead in Arnold's next picture at Paramount, huh? Deal?

PAUL: No problem, I've got Arnold on a string.

WAITER: (French accent) Gentlemen? I'm your waiter, Roman.

PAUL: Hello, Roman.

WAITER: And the endangered catch of the day is porpoise.

PAUL: Well, ah, how do you serve it?

WAITER: We don't. You pay for it and we give the money to Greenpeace.

PAUL: I'll have it.

GEORGE: Yeah, and I'll have what he's having.

ALEX: (approaching) George, Paul.

GEORGE: Alex!

PAUL: Daaaarling…

ALEX: Aha…what are my two favorite bad boys plotting today?

PAUL: Hey, it's not in your court, Alex. It's a matter of the heart.

ALEX: Paul, in my court, love is nothing.

GEORGE: *Touche'!* (all laugh) How's Femme Advertising?

ALEX: Oh, you didn't see *Ad Rag* today? I acquired the Milano Fatale Agency. I'm "Femme-Fatale" now…

PAUL: Oh, I see you're having a whale for lunch.

ALEX: What? Oh, that's Herr Trigger.

GEORGE: (laughs) That bozo is the German pistol magnate?

ALEX: My very latest client. I am going to make his little guns very, very big.

GEORGE: Ooooh…

ALEX: I'm going to turn him around.

PAUL: Good, good, Alex, you turn him around. You part his hair, paint a couple of eyes on the back of his head, and he'll be a real looker.

JOCELYN: Mr. Power, Mr. Power? Telephone.

PAUL: Oh, thank you, Jocelyn. Excuse me. (HE LEAVES)

GEORGE: So, Alexandra, sit down, sit down.

ALEX: Thanks, George.

GEORGE: Are we we still on for tonight?

ALEX: What about your—ah—wife?

GEORGE: She's gutting the house.

ALEX: Again?

GEORGE: Yeah, she's got a new favorite color.

JOCELYN: Ms. Femme, telephone.

ALEX: Excuse me, George.

PAUL: Hurry back…

ALEX: Meryl—You hermit! Jane, eat, eat… Madonna! Nice, ah, nice workout outfit…

JOCELYN: Ms. Femme?

ALEX: Thank you, Jocelyn. Hello?

PAUL: (on filter) Alex?

ALEX: Paul?

PAUL: (on filter) Are we—happening—tonight?

ALEX: What about your—ah—wife?

PAUL: (on filter) Astrid? She's in betrayal therapy.

ALEX: Whatever for?

PAUL: (on filter) She thinks—I'm having an affair!

ALEX: (She laughs and Paul joins in)

MFX: END TECHNO THEME OUT.

POWER #2: DRIVING MR. POWER

SFX: THEME OUT, SEQUE TO INTERIOR CAR UNDER

PAUL: Thanks for the lift home, George.

GEORGE: Glad to help, Paul, any time.

PAUL: Hey, my car is down at the clinic for its physical…

GEORGE: Again?

PAUL: Yeah, again. Well, any news?

GEORGE: Yes, yes, a little bit. I talked with your wife.

PAUL: Better than I can do. Does Astrid still want a separation?

GEORGE: Oh, yeah. But I made some progress.

PAUL: Hmmm?

GEORGE: Yeah, She's going to keep her name on the joint bank account.

PAUL: Well, what about the custody situation?

GEORGE: She wants every other weekend with your inner child.

PAUL: Oh, she does, huh?

GEORGE: Uh-huh.

PAUL: Well, George, I talked to the child within me…

GEORGE: Really…?

PAUL: Yeah, and he's getting his own lawyer.

GEORGE: *Legalorum trenchio, arbis pecuniam bandini.*

PAUL: Huh?

GEORGE: "Plant a lawyer, grow a money tree." (laughs) New Latin.

SFX: HELICOPTER PASSES OVERHEAD

PAUL: Hey, hey, what kind of a chopper is that?

GEORGE: What? Lemme get the window down here…

SFX: CAR WINDOW

PAUL: Police? News? Fruit fly spraying?

GEORGE: No, no, no—that's Marcie! Hi, Marcie! My wife. I told you she was gutting the house.

PAUL: Yeah, yeah...

GEORGE: Well, she's going Santa Fe in a big way. Look, look— she's flying in boulders from Sedona for the waterfall in the bedroom.

PAUL: I envy you. George. I envy your impossible life. I yearn for your impossible schedule.

GEORGE: Come off it, Paul. You're impossibly busy, too.

PAUL: Yeah, yeah, busy, busy, busy, building and breaking people. But, but what about me? I got a hole in my life big enough to drop a boulder through. Hey, Marcie! Right here!

GEORGE: No, no, no, don't do that, don't do that—she may do it. Are you trying to tell me you got some kind of a real problem you haven't told me about?

PAUL: George—I can't get it up.

GEORGE: Oh, my God. Have you thought about the pump?

PAUL: The... pump?

GEORGE: The potency pump; the male organ implant.

PAUL: No, no, no, you don't get it.

GEORGE: I don't need it.

PAUL: Ha. I'm talking about the down.

GEORGE: What?

PAUL: The down, George. It's the down that's got me down. I can't get it up.

GEORGE: You can't get what up?

PAUL: I can't get the down up. Marvin Davis wants forty down for Twentieth.

GEORGE: You're going to buy Twentieth Century Fox?

PAUL: It's the only way I can get Marvin's parking place.

GEORGE: Paul, Paul, buddy—if you make a big move like that...

PAUL: Yeah, it's a big one.

GEORGE: …before you settle with Astrid, she's gonna own half that parking place.

PAUL: Ooooh, yeah…

GEORGE: Think about it.

SFX: PHONE RINGS – PICKS UP

GEORGE: Excuse me.

OILY: (Swedish accent, on filter) Oily Bombhoist here. I must speak with Mr. Power.

PAUL: Oh, it's my mechanic, George. Yeah, Oily, Power here—what's the prognosis?

OILY: (on filter) How are you Mr. Power?

PAUL: I'm fine. How's the car?

OILY: (on filter) Well, I got the cat scan on your car right here. (speaks Swedish, off) Okay. Aha, *ja*. There's good news and bad news.

PAUL: Give me the bad news.

OILY: (on filter) Okay. We got a problem in the motherboard of Your Smart Car computer system, *ja*.

PAUL: So, what's the good news?

OILY: (on filter) We're going to make a fortune fixin' it! Hahahaha! (speaks Swedish again)

PAUL: Oily? What exactly is the problem?

OILY: (on filter) Ah, let's see… your ignition system is listening to your radio, *ja*.

PAUL: So?

OILY: (on filter) *Ja,* well, you punch up the wrong station, and it could slam dance into another car, *ja.*

PAUL: What about the squeak in the back?

OILY: Just the gerbil in the tailpipe, *ja.*

PAUL: Okay, Oily, just fix the car before the end of the model year.

OILY: (on filter) *Ja, ja da,*I will do it, Mr. Power.

PAUL: Ten-four.

OILY: (on filter) Be good, now.

PAUL: (sighs) Oh, my…

GEORGE: Here's your house, Paul.

SFX: CAR STOPS, BRAKE ON

PAUL: Thanks, George.

GEORGE: You want me to pick you up tomorrow morning, you think?

PAUL: Phew! What's that stink?

GEORGE: Beats me.

SFX: BIRD SOUNDS IN BACKGROUND

SOLLY: (runs up) Dad! Dad, dad—Oh, hi, Mr. Scoff.

PAUL: Solly, Solly, what in the world is that smell, son?

SOLLY: It's Astrid, Dad.

PAUL: Oh, no, is she endorsing another of those cockamamie perfumes?

SOLLY: No, no—cowabunga! She came home from the Animal Rights benefit, right? And she had this, like, this funny look in her eyes, right? And, well, she's, she's burning all of her fur coats in the backyard.

PAUL: I hate the smell of ocelot in the evening!

MFX: POWER THEME OUT

POWER #3: ABSOLUTE STEEL

MFX: UPBEAT MUZAK IN BACKGROUND

SFX: SPORTS CLUB AMBIANCE

FEMALE: (on filter over PA system,) Hi, Guys, this is Lisa. Just to remind you that Happy Hour at the Healthy Wealthy Club will kick off at the Nature Boy Bar right after No Impact Aerobics. See ya there!

GEORGE: Hey, Bosco.

BOSCO: Yo, Mr. Scoff. Hey, I know you are a lawyer, but are those briefs legal? (laughs)

GEORGE: I leave my suits in the office, Bosco.

BOSCO: You lookin' good.

GEORGE: I'm feeling good.

BOSCO: Hey, have you been pumping iron?

GEORGE: No, it's silicone. I just had my thighs sucked, my butt tucked, my pecks pumped and my lips tightened.

BOSCO: You be one buff dude, lawyer Scoff.

GEORGE: *Merci.*

BOSCO: Hey, you want to suck up a health drink?

GEORGE: Yeah, what have you got?

BOSCO: I've got a B-1 and brandy. I got a Rum and rosehips. I got Gin and Ginseng.

GEORGE: All right, a G&G—make it a double.

PAUL: (enters) Are you George Scoff?

GEORGE: What? Yes...

PAUL: Get up slowly, Mr. Scoff.

GEORGE: Okay, okay, okay...

PAUL: Put both hands on the bar...

GEORGE: Yeah?

PAUL: And spread 'em.

GEORGE: Oh, oh, hey, is there a pro—problem, officer?

PAUL: Yes, sir, I'm busting you on a 1099.

GEORGE: Oh? What's a 1099?

PAUL: Failure to recognize your best friend impersonating a policeman.

GEORGE: Paul, oh, I thought it was you. Nice costume.

PAUL: Hey, hope I didn't hang you up, George.

GEORGE: Naw, you filled me out. I took an extra half hour of elective surgery, eh? What do you think, eh?

PAUL: Looking good.

GEORGE: Feeling good.

PAUL: Yeah, I'm feeling lousy, George. I was pulled over in Beverly Hills for driving a car under fifty thousand.

GEORGE: What are you talking about? Your Rolls is worth ten times that.

PAUL: Yeah, it's still in the shop. Oily's doing a triple bypass on the fuel line. I was driving my son's car.

GEORGE: Yeah, so you got a thirty-day warning.

PAUL: Uh, uh, I got a two-year option.

GEORGE: What?

PAUL: You see, this young Beverly Hills cop pulls me over and we start schmoozing, and, you know, next thing you know, we had a dynamite cop show concept. We traded uniforms; he's over at Disney pitching it to Katzenberg right now.

GEORGE: You're too much.

PAUL: I think I can get him a three-year overall and ten points.

GEORGE: Okay! Bosco? Give him a vodka and blood tonic.

PAUL: Oh, Bosco, hold the vodka. I'm on duty. (they laugh) So, George, did you talk to my lovely wife, Astrid?

GEORGE: Yeah. (sips) Yum, nice G&G… She's hired a new lawyer.

PAUL: Oh, who is it this time? Melvin Belli, Gloria Allred?

GEORGE: Try Perry Mason.

PAUL: Whew! That's heavy, Perry Mason? Wait…wait a
            minute. He's still on television?

GEORGE: No, it's on hiatus; he's working for her now.

PAUL: Who put the idea in her head?

GEORGE: Well, she said it was Judge Wopner.

PAUL: Astrid is divorcing me; Wopner doesn't do "Divorce
            Court."

GEORGE: I know that, they have the same betrayal therapist,
            remember?

PAUL: Oh, that's the kook that told her to burn her fur coats
            to make amends for all the little animal murders.
            Well, it could be worse.

GEORGE: Yeah, it's gonna be.

PAUL: Huh?

GEORGE: Astrid's booked on Oprah tomorrow.

PAUL: She's going public with our private life?

GEORGE: Well, not exactly. The theme of the show is, "Women
            Divorcing Tax Evaders."

PAUL: Oh, no, I gotta stop her.

MFX: MUSICAL DOOR CHIMES TRANSITION

ALEX: (OFF) Just a minute.

SFX: DOOR OPENS

ALEX: Oh!

GEORGE: (as a cop) Are you Alex Femme, the President of the Femme Fetal Agency?

ALEX: Femme Fatale. Yes, is there a problem, officer?

GEORGE: All right, Miss Femme. Put your hands against the wall and assume the position.

ALEX: Which one?

GEORGE: Don't get smart. I'm taking you in on a 1099.

ALEX: What's that?

GEORGE: Failing to recognize your sexually aroused lover in a policeman's uniform three sizes too small.

ALEX: (laughing) George, is that a warrant in your pocket, or are you just breaking and entering?

GEORGE: Let me get out of this uniform, Alex…

ALEX: No, wait! I've got a better idea. I'll slip into my Little Red Riding Hood outfit and you can bust me for carrying wine to Grandma's.

GEORGE: Oh, you bring out the Big Bad Wolf in me, baby.

SFX: KISSING UNDER NEXT SEGMENT

ALEX: George, did you tell Paul about Astrid going on Oprah?

GEORGE: Oh, Yeah, he's really upset. He thinks it could destroy him.

ALEX: I think that's what she wants.

GEORGE: Lexy, you could talk her out of it.

ALEX: Maybe, but the ratings on this "Oprah" are going
             to be astronomical, and six of my clients' ads are
             bookending her segment. My hands are tied.

GEORGE: Not yet…

SFX: HE HANDCUFFS HER

GEORGE: …leave that to me.

ALEX: If you make the handcuffs real tight, officer, I'll
             swallow the key.

GEORGE: Anything you say can be used against you. (they laugh
             together)

MFX: SHOW THEME IN AND OUT

POWER #4: DIAL P FOR POWER

SFX: UPSCALE BOUTIQUE AMBIANCE, PIANO IN BG

GEORGE: Paul, you don't look too—too great.

PAUL: I'm not feelin' too great either.

GEORGE: It's been a week now, hasn't it, since your wife filed for divorce?

PAUL: Yeah.

GEORGE: I mean, have you heard anything from Astrid at all?

PAUL: No, George, but who knows, man—she could be with her Medicine Blanket Meditation group in the high desert at one of those Jackalope Encounters.

GEORGE: Could be…

PAUL: Or she could be going around the world a couple of times in the Concorde.

GEORGE: Sure.

PAUL: She's done that before.

GEORGE: Yeah. Did you check the sensory deprivation tanning tank at home?

PAUL: First thing.

GEORGE: Hmmm.

21

PAUL: I don't have a good feeling about this, George.

GEORGE: (sighs) Paul, maybe…

PAUL: What?

GEORGE: Now just maybe—hear me out—maybe she realized that going on the *Woman Divorcing Tax Evaders* segment of Oprah could have done you serious harm.

PAUL: That doesn't sound like Astrid.

GEORGE: What I'm trying to say, Paul, is that maybe her heart is in the right place.

PAUL: In the sense that it's in the upper left quadrant of her chest. Look, Astrid missed more than going on the Oprah show. She missed two betrayal therapy appointments, a facial, a teeth bleaching, a leg waxing and an animal rights rally.

GEORGE: Oooh.

PAUL: I don't like it.

GEORGE: Do you like this?

PAUL: Uh, what?

GEORGE: These ties.

PAUL: Well, yeah, they're okay.

GEORGE: Yeah—Jacques!

JACQUES: *Oui, monsieur.*

GEORGE: I'll take these four ties.

JACQUES: You want a gift wrap-ped?

GEORGE: No, no—just attach them to my wrists and ankles and I'll wear them out. Kidding! Bag 'em.

SFX: BEEPER SOUNDS

PAUL: Ah—George, is that your phone or mine?

GEORGE: It's yours, Paul. Mine vibrates.

PAUL: Oh, yeah, yeah, just a second. Power here. What? You did? Well, can I talk to…? No, no, no, no, I'm listening.

GEORGE: What is it?

PAUL: Shhhhh! "Switch—switch 67 at the Union Pacific yard?" Yeah, yeah, yeah, I understand. Look, can I have—hello?

GEORGE: Paul?

PAUL: Hello?

GEORGE: Paul, what's goin' on?

PAUL: It's—Astrid.

GEORGE: You talked with Astrid?

PAUL: No, she's been kidnapped.

GEORGE: Oh, my God!

PAUL: The ransom instructions are under switch 67 in the Union Pacific train yard.

GEORGE: Well, let's go!

PAUL   Wait a minute. Are the train yards in Beverly Hills?

GEORGE: No, no, no, they're East of here.

PAUL: East of here? I've never been East of Beverly Hills…

GEORGE: Well, neither have I. I mean, we'll use your map book.

PAUL: I tore those pages out. I never thought I'd need them.

GEORGE: I'll drive. I've got a map program in my car computer, okay?

PAUL: Wait a minute. What if someone sees me leaving Beverly Hills going East?

GEORGE   You can lie on the back seat, okay? I'll cover you with that old blanket.

PAUL: What if they see you? They know you're my friend and they'll just figure that. . .

GEORGE: Now wait, now, wait, Paul—I'll go in disguise, OK? Jacques!

JACQUES: (COMING ON) *Oui, oui, monsieur Scoff.*

GEORGE: Give me that moustache over there on that manikin.

JACQUES: *Le—le moustache?*

GEORGE: Yes, I want the moustache. Take it off, I'll pay anything!

JACQUES: *Oui!* (exiting) *Toute Suite!* Ah, these crazy Americans…

GEORGE: Hurry!

JACQUES: Crazy...

MFX: NERVOUS TECHNO MUSIC TAG OUT

POWER #5: MURDERING THE ORIENT EXPRESS

MFX: TECHO TERROR CHORD

SFX: FOOTSTEPS ON RAILYARD GRAVEL, TRAIN WHISTLE
      IN B.G.

PAUL: (coming on) Sixty-three, sixty-five…

GEORGE: Sixty-six.

BOTH: Sixty-seven!

PAUL: Here we are.

GEORGE: And there's the switch.

PAUL: Yeah.

GEORGE: I don't see a note, though. Do you see any—?

PAUL: Well, maybe if I—um—move the switch, George.

GEORGE: No, no, I don't think you should move that switch.

PAUL: C'mon, George, we're talking about a situation that
          could affect my—(efforts) re-pu-tation! There!

GEORGE: There it is, there it is!

PAUL: There it is! Give it to me.

GEORGE: Here.

PAUL: Give it to me, quick!

26

GEORGE: Hey, we better get off the track; here comes a train.

SFX: HORRENDOUS DERAILMENT AND CRASH — FIRE AND EXPLOSIONS CONTINUE UNDER

PAUL: Oh, God, that's horrible!

GEORGE: All the humanity!

PAUL: No, not the train, George, the note!

GEORGE: Oh…

PAUL: Listen to this: "Paul, I am being held hostage by the Bow-Wowists…"

GEORGE: The Bow-Wowists? That's the Radical Animal Right!

PAUL: Yeah. "If you want to see me in one piece again"— hmmmm…

GEORGE: What is it?

PAUL: I'm not sure I want to see her in one piece again.

GEORGE: Paul! Paul, if you don't try to save her, you'll be the most hated man in Hollywood.

PAUL: Oh. Well—I already am.

GEORGE: I mean, in a negative way.

PAUL: Oh. Well, OK, there're three demands.

GEORGE: All right, read 'em.

PAUL: "One: make twenty million dollars available to the Bow-Wowist cause."

GEORGE: Twenty mil!

PAUL: Oh, yeah—hmmm…

GEORGE: That's—it's deductable.

SFX: FIRE TRUCK SIRENS IN B.G. UNDER

PAUL: OK, I can live with it, alright. "Two: Release Lassie from his contract." Hey!

GEORGE: You sweated blood to get that collie to shake hands!

PAUL: Yeah, if I let him out, George, he's gonna walk across the street to William Morris. I can smell it!

GEORGE: Well, you may have to live with that one. Go ahead, what's—what's the third one?

PAUL: Third. let's see. "You will produce this kidnapping as a Movie-of-the-Week." (starts laughing. George joins in) An M-O-W!

GEORGE: (laughing) No!

PAUL: C'mon!

GEORGE: I don't believe it!

PAUL: Well, let's see, let's see—Okay, wait a minute, okay, let's see… Fade in…

GEORGE: Exterior train yard…

PAUL: Train yard, day.

GEORGE: Day!

PAUL: Okay—The camera swoops down to find Paul Power, a handsome man in his late forties…

GEORGE: Thirties.

PAUL: All right, thirties.

GEORGE: Sure, why not?

PAUL: Standing—ah—reading a ransom note…

GEORGE: Unison) Reading a ransom note… uh-huh.

PAUL: Towering over his companion, George Scoff…

GEORGE: Wait a minute, wait a minute. Hey, hey, Paul! What do you mean "towering"? This is nonsense! what're we talking about? What proof do we have that they've even GOT her?

PAUL: Proof? Right here, George. It's her—finger!

GEORGE: Those butchers!!

PAUL: Her, her fingernail, George! She's always breaking them…

MFX: DRAMATIC TECHO CHORD

POWER #6: THE FIRM

SFX: INTERIOR SCOFF LAW WAITING ROOM – PHONE RINGS

SANDY: Scoff Law. George Scoff's office. (Admiral on filter throughout) Oh, Admiral Poindexter, Mr. Scoff was expecting your call. We need your new address for the billing.—Federal Low Security Compound—Penthouse Suite C.—Fort Daiseychain, California, Penthouse C. Isn't that next door to Jim Baker? —Oh, it's Zsa Zsa! There goes the neighborhood.—Hold on, Admiral, Mr. Scoff wants to say hello.

SFX: OFFICE AMBIANCE OUT

GEORGE: So, Paul, tell me, did you let Lassie go?

PAUL: Yeah, George, I let him out of his leash.

GEORGE: Doggone.

SFX: INTERCOM BUZZER

GEORGE: Excuse me.

SANDY: (on filter) Admiral P. on three.

GEORGE: I'll just be a second, Paul. (on phone) Admiral, all battened down and shipshape, sir.—Good. Good. I just wanted to say: twelve felony counts, six months?—Looking good! Ha, ha, ha, ha, Merry Christmas.—Yes, sir. (hangs up) What a guy.

PAUL: Oh, Lassie. Lassie. I got him on my mind. I turned that mutt into a billion-dollar bitch, and now he's across the street eating out of William Morris' hand.

GEORGE: Well, you had no choice. If you want to see your wife again you've got to do what these Bow-Wowists tell you.

PAIL: Who are these Bow-Wowists anyway?

GEORGE: I had a couple of my paralegals research it...

SFX: PAPER SHUFFLING

GEORGE: Let's see—they're the newest group to come out of the Radical Animal Right. They have this wacky idea that animals shouldn't be exploited for commercial purposes.

PAUL: What next, huh?

GEORGE: Well, up to now they've been breaking into laboratories and liberating white rats and bunny rabbits.

PAUL: Well, they sound like Astrid's kind of people.

GEORGE: Could be, you know, the Stockholm Syndrome...

PAUL: No.

GEORGE: The kidnappee identifying with the kidnappers.

PAUL: You think she might fall for one of these creeps?

GEORGE: Ummm...

PAUL: Gee, then I wouldn't have to pay alimony.

GEORGE: That's not exactly what I meant, Paul.

SFX: INTERCOM BEEP

GEORGE: Excuse me. What is it, Sandy?

SANDY: (on filter) Mr. Scoff, Neil Bush is here with "the bag."

GEORGE: Okay, tell him to put it in the regular place. And the envelope...

SANDY: (on filter) Yes?

GEORGE: ...is for his dad.

SANDY: Oh, yes, sir.

GEORGE: Well, you still have to come up with that, what, twenty-million-dollar ransom? That's demand number two...

PAUL: What?

GEORGE: No, number one.

PAUL: I'm going to cover that. I've got a meeting with my stockbroker.

GEORGE: Who are you with now?

PAUL: Same, guy, Ivan Bosky.

POWER#7: BOSKY'S BACK

SFX: INTERIOR WAREHOUSE AMBIANCE — FOOTSTEPS
APPROACH, VOICES ON ECHO.

BOSKY: Paul, Paul, I'm over here. Ha-ha. Grab that crate, drag
it on over and sit down. My apologies for the office, I
haven't had a chance to gussy it up yet.

PAUL: Nice warehouse you got here.

BOSKY: I need the space after all those months cooped up in
that…well, you know. Don't worry, this place is going
to look great. I'm getting a lot of stuff from Trump's
Taj.

PAUL: So, Ivan, how does it feel to be back on the street?

BOSKY: I'm a changed man. Look at me. See the grey hair, the
beard? The Howard Hughes look. "Ivan The Terrible."
You like it?

PAUL: What's not to like? It's you.

BOSKY: It's me! (laughs) So, how can I help you?

PAUL: I want you to refer me to a ruthless, bottom line, no-
questions-asked stockbroker.

BOSKY: You're looking at him.

PAUL: Ivan, if I remember correctly, when you copped the plea with the Feds, they took your license away.

BOSKY: They took away the license of Ivan BOSKEY with an 'e'. Look at this letterhead.

PAUL: Ivan Bosky.

BOSKY: No 'e'.

PAUL: No 'e'.

BOSKY: Heh? Let's talk.

PAUL: Okay, Bosky, no 'e', I want you to liquidate my twenty million dollars worth of junk bonds.

BOSKY: (laughs) I got you out of junk bonds into something more conservative.

PAUL: What? T-Bills? CDs?

BOSKY: Suicide machines.

PAUL: What!

BOSKY: You're going to make a killing—so to speak.

PAUL: You invested me in suicide machines?

BOSKY: Yeah, Kervorkian, Dr. Death, the Volkswagen—you know, "Oldtimers' Disease." You forget to kill yourself, the machine does it for you.

PAUL: You mean I'm sitting on top of twenty million dollars worth of suicide machines?

BOSKY: No, no, you're sitting on *one*. Open the crate.

SFX: CRATE IS OPENED

BOSKY: Go on, go on, it's a gift. Put it in the trunk of your car.

PAUL: Well, what am I going to do with it?

BOSKY: You get stuck in one of those traffic jams, and you can't take it—you've got it, eh? Heh, heh, heh, heh…

MFX: TECHNO CHORD OUT

POWER #8: RUGRAT PATROL

MFX: TANGO THEME UP AND UNDER

SFX: RESTAURANT AMBIANCE

> HERR T: (German accent) So, Alex, how are you handling my gun?

> ALEX: With kid gloves, Herr Trigger.

> HERR T: Hmmm.

> ALEX: I have found the perfect niche for your automatic weapons.

> HERR T: Oh?

> ALEX: Children's television.

> HERR T: Children's television? *Gotterdamerung!* If Adolph had had children's television, we'd all be speaking with funny accents like mine.

> ALEX: It gets better. Development came up with this...

> HERR T: What's this, a box of cereal?

SFX: CEREAL POURED INTO BOWL

> HERR T: Oh, no! Special A-K!

> ALEX: Bite-sized assault rifles.

HERR T: We'll make a cereal killing! *Wunderbar!*

ALEX: Milk?

HERR T: *Ja wohl.*

ALEX: Stand back…

SFX: MILK POURED. TINY GUNFIRE.

ALEX: Better than "snap, crackle, pop", huh?

HERR T: Alex—you genius! You have given me the children of
            the world. What can I give you?

ALEX: Well…

HERR T: Anything—the Donald's yacht? The Fuerher's nest?

SFX: MOBILE PHONE BEEP

MALE S'CT: (British, on filter) Ms. Femme?

ALEX: What is it, Sandy?

S'CT: Paul Power is here to see you.

ALEX: Thank you. Herr trigger, I know what I want.

HERR T: Anything.

ALEX: How about a loan—for twenty million dollars?

HERR T: Ge-done.

ALEX: Ahaaaa. (laughs politely)

MFX: TECHO CYMBAL CRASH

ALEX: Paul, I've never seen you looking so powerless, so pale. Is it a new talcum powder or are you in trouble?

PAUL: It shows, huh?

ALEX: Yes…

PAUL: You know, Alex, maybe we shouldn't jet down to T.J. for the bullfights, tonight.

ALEX: You came all the way over here to tell me that? You could've faxed me.

PAUL: Alex, I need a favor.

ALEX: Yes?

PAUL: A big favor.

ALEX: Oooh, I love giving big favors.

PAUL: I need twenty million dollars.

ALEX: You still trying to buy Murdoch's parking place at Fox?

PAUL: No! I need it for my wife.

ALEX: Why, Paul, whatever is possessing you—the spirit of Richard Burton?

PAUL: Alex, I'm not buying her anything worthwhile. I'm buying Astrid her freedom.

ALEX: Oh! And she's settling for twenty mil? She must really want out.

PAUL: Alex! I'm not talking about a divorce settlement, alright? Astrid's been kidnapped by the Bow-Wowists.

ALEX: Those animal rights kooks? I just lost the Dead Dog
           Cat Food account over them. What a campaign—"a
           full pound—

PAUL: (under) Alex…

ALEX: —of ground round pound hound—

PAUL: Alex…

ALEX: —in every can!"

PAUL: Alex! I'm going to lose a lot more than a stupid cat
           food account if I don't come up with that twenty-
           million-dollar ransom.

ALEX: Paul, you don't have to come to me. Liquidate some
           stocks.

PAUL: Yeah, I just came from Bosky. He's put my whole
           portfolio into suicide futures.

ALEX: Not the Kervorkian Machine?

PAUL: Yes—the Kervorkian Machine. (SINGS) "Push a
           button: drip-drip, snore, ya don't have to deal with life
           no more."

ALEX: Paul, that's good! Lemme write it down.

PAUL: Yeah, but until the court lifts the injunction on that
           little beauty, my stocks are as frozen as Walt Disney.

ALEX: Listen, pal, you want twenty million—you've got it.

PAUL: Oh, Alex! What can I say?

ALEX: Well, let's say ten points over prime…

PAUL: Ten points?

ALEX: Your agency as collateral...

PAUL: My agency?

ALEX: And payback in five days.

PAUL: Five days!

ALEX: All right—a week.

PAUL: Well, you've got me over a barrel.

ALEX: Hmmm, not yet—but we could try that tonight. (sexy laugh))

POWER #9: THE GREATEST STORY EVER SOLD

MFX: FEMALE CHORUS SINGS THE NBC CHIMES

PAUL: Brandon, we've known each other since Yale.

TART: That's right, Paulie, we have.

PAUL: Boola, Boola.

TART: Boola, Boola. Boola, Boola.

PAUL: So I didn't feel uncomfortable—

TART: No.

PAUL: Coming down here like this, unannounced.

TART: No, no, no, come in anytime.

PAUL: Uh, I feel I can confide in you.

TART: You can, you can do that.

PAUL: Even if you are the President of NBC Television.

TART: I am, I am the President of NBC Television. Hold it a
            second, Paulie. Ah, Sandy?

SANDY: (on filter) Yes, Mr. Tartikov.

TART: Hold all calls. I'm being confided in.

SANDY: (on filter) Yes, Mr. Tartikov.

41

TART: You were saying, Paul.

PAUL: Brandon, my—ah—wife has been kidnapped by terrorists.

TART: I like it.

PAUL: I knew you would, that's why I brought it to you first.

SFX: INTERCOM BEEP

SANDY: (on filter) Mr. Tartikov, are you still being confided in?

TART: Yes, I am, Sandy.

SANDY: (on filter) I have Bill Cosby on one, Alf on two and Kristie Alley on three.

TART: Oh—put Alf on with Kristie, he's a big fan.

SANDY: (on filter) Yes, Mr. Tartikov.

TART: What does "The Cos" want?

SANDY: (on filter) He's very upset. He read a review that said his show was about a black family.

TART: So?

SANDY: (on filter) He's threatening to go to Ted Turner and be de-colorized.

TART: Thank you, Sandy. You see what I'm up against, Paul? Being head of NBC is seven days a week dealing with peacocks.

PAUL: Why don't you just replace Cosby with Alf, Brandon?

TART: Oh, we tested that. Stuffed animals and puppets loved it; but we missed Middle America.

PAUL: What's the difference?

TART: Okay, okay, I'll work it out. Pitch me your MOW.

PAUL: Let me give you the *TV Guide* on it.

TART: Do it to me.

PAUL: The beautiful wife of Paul Power, Hollywood's premier agent, is held hostage by radical animal rightists. He has to make this Movie of The Week to get her back alive.

TART: Paul, that's brilliant. What are you going to call it?

PAUL: "Bad Dog."

TART: Oh! I love it. I give you the green light on the MOW and you get your MIA back.

PAUL: Brandon, think of the ratings.

TART: Oh!

PAUL: Think of the demographics! Run it opposite *The Simpsons* and you'll bury Bart.

TART: Forget the numbers, forget the business, this is a matter of saving my dear friend's wife. More than that, what do I need? I need Schwarzenneger to play you and Madonna to play your wife.

PAUL: Well, I'm not sure…

TART: Well, I'm very busy, Paul. My regards to the wife.

PAUL: Give me the phone, Brandon.

SFX: GRABS PHONE

TART: That's better.

SFX: PHONE TONES

ARNOLD: (on filter) *Ja*, speak.

PAUL: Arnie? Paul.

ARNOLD: (on filter) Thousand three, thousand four...

PAUL: Put down the weights, Arnie.

ARNOLD: (on filter) ... thousand five, okay.

SFX: WEIGHTS DROPPED

ARNOLD: (on filter) *Wie geht es*, Paul?

PAUL: Arnie, I'm in Brandon Tartikov's office.

ARNOLD: (on filter) Hello, Brandon.

TART: Hello, Big Boy. How was your trip to Mars?

ARNOLD: (on filter) I can't remember. (THEY ALL LAUGH)

PAUL: Arnie, Arnie, clear the slate, I've just signed you in a very important Movie of The Week to play me.

ARNOLD: (on filter) Paul...

PAUL: Yes.

ARNOLD: (on filter) I did lunch today at Spago with Wolfie and Lassie...

PAUL: Arnold, I can explain.

ARNOLD: (on filter) You don't have to. I got it right from the doggie's mouth. You kicked him out of your stable.

PAUL: You're mixing your metaphors, Arnie.

ARNOLD: (on filter) I can't understand your motivation, Paul, throwing away such a high-priced talent.

PAUL: Okay, Arnie, I can tell you what's behind all this, but you're going to have to keep it a secret.

ARNOLD: (on filter) *Da stimpt.* Quiet, everybody, I'm being told a secret.

CROWD: (on filter, off) "A secret, a secret, Arnie's got a secret."

PAUL: I had to let Lassie go in order to save my wife, Astrid's life.

ARNOLD: (on filter) Hmmm, I see. You made a decision of the heart.

PAUL: I knew you'd understand.

ARNOLD: (on filter) I do. I do. We're through. I'll send the truck over in the morning to get my pictures.

SFX: CROWD SHOUTS THEIR SUPPORT IN THE BACKGROUND

PAUL: Arnie! Arnie!

SFX: PHONE DIAL TONE

TART: Well, Paul, I don't have to be Dick Tracy to guess what Madonna's going to say…

MFX: COMIC TECHNO TAG

POWER #10: NIGHTMARE ON VINE STREET

SANDY: Mr. Powers, why won't you let us open the office? The lobby is jammed with clients trying to get in.

PAUL: They're not trying to get in, Sandy, they're trying to get OUT.

JACK: (coming on) Paul? Can I talk to you?

PAUL: Oh, Nicholson, I'm awfully busy right now. Could you come back in a coupla jakes?

JACK: This'll only take a second. I quit!

PAUL: Jack, you joker! Jack, Jack! Come back!

KATE: Man, get out of my way! Mr. Power…

PAUL: Ms. Hepburn!

KATE: The word on the street is that you're sinking, and this is one ship I am not going down with.

PAUL: But Katherine…

KATE: Don't Bogart that contract, my friend, pass it over to me.

SFX: RIPS UP CONTRACT

SLY: Yo, Katie! Way to go!

PAUL: No, not you, too, Sly!

SLY: Call me Sylvester. Only my agent calls me Sly.

PAUL: I AM your agent…

SLY: And they call *me* stupid! Ha!

MM: (Whispery) Paul…Paul…

PAUL: Who's that?

MM: Oh, Paul…

PAUL: Is that really you, Marilyn?

MM: Yes—and I want out.

PAUL: But…you *are* out. You're dead.

MM: No, Paul—You're dead (on echo) dead—dead—
            dead—dead (fades out)

PAUL: Arrrrggghhhh! Ah, ah—oh, oh, oh—it was—it was
            just a celebrity impersonators' nightmare!

SFX: PHONE RINGS

PAUL: Oh, it's three in the morning, what now?

SFX: PICKS UP PHONE.

VOICE: (On filter) Bow wow, bow wow.

PAUL: Oh, no…

VOICE   (On filter) Bow wow.

PAUL: Oh, noooooooooooo!

POWER #11: ON THE BEACH

SFX: BEACH AMBIANCE. EARLY MORNING

GEORGE: (Breathing hard) Paul, Paul, slow up.

PAUL: Okay, okay.

GEORGE: You aren't running for your life here.

PAUL: It sure feels like it, George,

GEORGE: I can't keep up with ya, I had some heavy tortes yesterday.

PAUL: In court?

GEORGE: No, no, after court at Godiva's Sugar Palace. The Amaretto Mousse Sludge just won't digest.

PAUL: Okay, okay, we'll walk for a while,

GEORGE: Oh, nice beach here in Santa Monica…

PAUL: Oh! George, look out for the hypodermic needles.

GEORGE: What? Those little shiny things? I thought They were just phosphorescent plankton stuff.

PAUL: Naw, that went out with the Red Tide.

GEORGE: Then what makes them glow?

PAUL: Low level hospital waste.

GEORGE: Oh, that's terrible.

PAUL: Well, not at night, George. You look out on the beach—a thousand points of light.

GEORGE: Heh, heh, heh. Hey, my wife showed me a headline in the trades today that read: "Bankables Ankle Power Pack."

PAUL: Yeah.

GEORGE: Yeah? Well, what does it mean?

PAUL: It means that my agency has become the Hubble telescope of Hollywood.

GEORGE: Huh?

PAUL: If you look in my office, you won't see any stars.

EORGE: Those Bow-Wowist kidnappers and their cockamamie demands, they're ruining you.

PAUL: There's nothing wrong with ruining a man. I mean, I do that every day, I'm a trained professional. But by ruining me, they're making it impossible to meet their other demands.

GEORGE: The Movie of the Week about the kidnapping.

PAUL: Yeah, something smells fishy.

GEORGE: That's the dead perch on this beach.

PAUL: Oh, yeah.

GEORGE: They've got so much mercury in them that when the temperature rises, they stand up and their heads turn red.

PAUL: Well, what am I going to do?

GEORGE: Well, I thought you took a meeting with your pal, Tartikov at NBC.

PAUL: Brandon and I were at Yale together,

GEORGE: (Sings) "Bah, bah, bah!"

PAUL: He was very sympathetic about saving my wife until I couldn't produce Schwarzenegger for the lead of The MOW.

GEORGE: What are you talking about? Arnold's your client.

PAUL: Yeah? He ankled.

GEORGE: Ankle implants? He'll be back on his feet in a few days.

PAUL: No, no, no, he *ankled*, George. He walked, he split, he skipped.

GEORGE: He left your agency?

PAUL: Yeah, followed by Nicholson, Willis, De Niro, Streep, Madonna, Fonda, Alf, Redford and Cruise.

GEORGE: God, have you got anybody left?

PAUL: Oh yeah, I've still got Andrew Dice Clay; but I have to waste a couple of hours on the phone every day talking dirty to him to keep him happy.

GEORGE: Well, what about the other networks?

PAUL: It's a club, George. If you've got the bread, you're upper crust. If you don't, you're toast.

GEORGE: Right.

PAUL: I tried CBS, ABC, F-O-X, the syndies, cable. Public access won't return my calls.

GEORGE: Oh, we got a real problem, Paul.

PAUL: Yeah, the Bow-Wowists are going to kill my wife, and the bad publicity is going to kill what's left of *me*.

GEORGE: This turn of events could kill our little agreement.

PAUL: What are you talking about?

GEORGE: Well, you know, I've been handling your divorce proceedings with Astrid in exchange for your promise to put my wife, Marcie, in Arnold's next movie.

PAUL: That's true.

GEORGE: Heh, heh, your bill's already in seven figures.

PAUL: Hey, don't worry, Georgie. Look, Dice Clay is the man of the hour, and I'm putting Marcie in his next film.

GEORGE: What's it about?

PAUL: Oh, what a concept, what a hook! Look, it's great; it's perfect for Marcy. It's the story of the woman behind the man who built the Panama Canal.

GEORGE: Oh, really? What's it called?

PAUL: "Ditch Bitch."

GEORGE: Huh! I don't know…

DWAYBE: (running up) Yo, dudes, cool your dogs, man. This beach is off limits from here all the way to Palos Verdes.

GEORGE: What's the problem...ah...

DWAYNE: Dwayne, man...lifeguard Dwayne. We've had another ecological event, you know. A purely spontaneous, traumatic encounter in the bay.

GEORGE: Oh, how should we feel about this?

DWAYNE: I'm totally bummed, *hombre*. I mean, remember that rogue garbage scow that cut loose in New York harbor last year?

GEORGE: It went down in the Straits of Magellan.

DWAYNE: No, *negativo*, man. El Nino kept it afloat and the Greenhouse thermal blew it north until this morning it collided with the Exxon Benedict Arnold.

GEORGE: Oh, no!

DWAYNE: It's Pampers in oil all the way to Catalina.

GEORGE: Thanks, Dude. We'll leave the beach,

DWAYNE: You can jog on the freeway, it's Gridlock City. (Running off) Later, *hombre*...

GEORGE: So long, ah, man.

PAUL: Walk me back to my stretch, George, would you? I've got a favor to ask you.

GEORGE: Yeah, my clock is on, I'll do anything I can.

PAUL: I'm delivering the twenty-million-dollar ransom to the Bow-Wowists tonight.

GEORGE: Twenty million. (giggles) Must have put a big hole in the Swiss.

PAUL: Uh uh.

GEORGE: Well, where did you come up with a bundle like that?

PAUL: Let's just say I went down to the laundry and turned in my ticket.

GEORGE: Hey, George, you're not ready to see the Bow-Wowists yet. You've got the money, but you haven't got the movie.

PAUL: That's where you come in, Georgie. Here, put on this moustache.

GEORGE: What?

PAUL: Just put it on.

GEORGE: Ha ha, okay—there.

PAUL: Perfect, you look just like him.

GEORGE: Oh, yeah, really? Just like who?

PAUL: The man who's going to make my movie—Ted Turner.

POWER #12: SEX LIVES ON VIDEOTAPE

SFX: RADIO AMBIANCE

REX: This is Rex Reed, with more delicious gossip from Tinsletown. Lassie's come out of the closet! It was hairdo to hairdo with Arsinio last night. Lassie is shedding the nice-puppy image to play the totally butch lead in "Bad Dog 2". Now get this! "Bad Dog 2" is the first sequel to be released *before* the original! The suits at Warner are gambling that "Bad Dog 2" will create a built-in audience for "Bad Dog 1" which isn't slated to be lensed and released until late 1992. One other note: before Lassie was shooed off the couch, she revealed that she's leaving her former agent, Paul Power, and say—who isn't? Poor Paul's really in the doghouse. (beat) Ivana Trump's complaining again. She jettisoned her Southerby's Van Gogh auction with her 25 million-dollar alimony check and could only afford a frame!

SFX: MOBILE PHONE RINGS/PICKUP

GEORGE: George Scoff, in transit.

ALEX: (on filter throughout) Alex Femme, in the shower. I'm wet and waiting. What's your ETA?

GEORGE: E-T-A?

ALEX: "Estimated Time of Adultery".

GEORGE: Aw, oh, sweetheart, I was just about to call you.

ALEX: Oh, good. I've been writing dirty limericks all over my body with the soap crayons you gave me.

GEORGE: Oh, stop it, you're hurting me.

ALEX: No, that's for later.

GEORGE: Oh, please, please, Alex, listen to me. Something's come up and we can't go to the Pit Bull Charity fight at Roseanne Barr's.

ALEX: Oh, too bad. And I gave her a better-than-even chance.

GEORGE: Yeah, but maybe I can come over later. You'll just love this costume.

ALEX: Disguise yourself, and I'll try you on the tileman— I mean, on the tile, man.

GEORGE: OK. I've got a very neatly trimmed grey-flecked moustache and a kind of silver-grey hair...

ALEX : Daddy!

GEORGE: And casually, but impeccably attired in a Mister Leisure of Atlanta pseudo-suede sailor suit.

ALEX: Are you going to a costume party as Ted Turner?

GEORGE: Oh, you're good!

ALEX: What's up, George?

GEORGE: Well, I guess I can tell you, Alex. I'm on my way to pick up Paul. We're meeting with his wife's kidnappers to turn over the ransom and meet the rest of their demands; and I'm going to convince them that Turner is going to produce their Movie of the Week.

ALEX: Well, good luck, Georgie.

GEORGE: Thanks.

ALEX: Come over later, and we'll see if your disguise holds water.

GEORGE: Ciao, baby...

MFX: EXIT STING

POWER #13: PET CEMETERY

SFX: INTERIOR CAR AMBIANCE

GEORGE: Are you sure we took the right exit, Paul? I haven't seen a sign in miles.

PAUL: There it is. See the balloons and the garage sale signs? Now, turn right. Now we just go straight along here until we see—there it is.

GEORGE: (reading) "Eternal Rest Pet Cemetery, Lost Our Lease, Everything Must Go, Come and Get 'Em."

PAUL: Pull over.

SFX: THEY EXIT THE CAR AND BEGIN WALKING

GEORGE: Got the money?

PAUL: Yeah.

GEORGE: Ow!

PAUL: What's the matter, George?

GEORGE: I stepped in a hole. Gimme the flashlight.

PAUL: Here.

GEORGE: Look at this, a little tombstone.

PAUL: What does it say?

GEORGIE: "In memory of—Ritchie our beloved gerbil. Loved you to the end."

PAUL: Be careful, George, there are holes everywhere.

GEORGE: Look at the size of that one. What does that stone say?

PAUL: "To Dumbo, we'll never forget you." That's touching.

BOWIST 1: (on voice-changer) Step down into the elephant's grave.

GEORGE: Elephant's grave—that's spooky.

PAUL: Don't forget your accent, Ted. We're coming!

THEY ADLIB AS THEY DESCEND INTO THE GRAVE

BOWIST 2: (on voice-changer) Who's that with you, Paul? We told you to come alone.

PAUL: Tell 'em.

GEORGE: Hi, y'all. I'm Ted Turner. CNN, TNT, USA?

BOWIST 1: (on voice-changer) You sound like Jimmy Carter.

GEORGE: You heard one Georgian, honey, you've heard us all—ah—y'all.

PAUL: You guys should talk; you don't even sound human.

GEORGE: They don't even look human.

BOWIST 2: (on voice-changer) We're talking through ultrasonic canine-callers implanted in our dog masks.

PAUL: Let's get this awful charade over with.

BOWIST 1:   (on voice-changer) Have you met our demands?

PAUL: Yes, here's Lassie's release, and here's the money,

BOWIST 2:   (on voice-changer) What about the Movie of the Week?

PAUL: Tell 'em, Ted.

GEORGE: Well, y'all, I brought this deal memo for y'all to sign so
             we can put this turkey up on the bird, y'all.

BOWIST 1:   (on voice-changer) Hand it over.

PAUL: Hold it a second, man's best friend. Before you get
             your paws on anything, you're going to have to prove
             to me that my wife is here and safe,

BOWIST 2:   (on voice-changer) That's easy. You see that
             rhinoceros' mausoleum over there?

PAUL: Ummm, yeah.

BOWIST 2:   (on voice-changer) Well, talk to her.

PAUL: Astrid, Astrid, can you hear me?

ASTRID: (distant) Paul, Paul, I'm all right , honey. Just do what
             they say.

BOWIST 1:   (on voice-changer) Satisfied?

PAUL: Okay, here's Lassie's release.

BOWIST 2:   (on voice-changer) That's his paw print, all right.

PAUL: And the money.

SFX: SUITCASE OPENED

BOWIST 1:   (on voice-changer) It's all here.

GEORGE: And here's the deal memo.

SFX: CONTRACT OPENED

BOWIST 1:   (on voice-changer) Haw! A memo from Turner? This is as phony as your moustache.

SFX: MOUSTACHE RIPPED OFF

GEORGE: Ow—y'all.

BOWIST 1:   (on voice-changer) Dart 'em!

SFX: BOTH ARE SHOT WITH DARTS

PAUL: Oh, no—elephant tranquilizer…

MFX: DESCENDING TECHO MUSIC OUT

POWER #14: PET CEMETERY II

SFX: DESCENDING ELECTRONIC EFFECT; BIRD CALLS IN B.G.

PAUL: (Snoring stops, coughs) Ohhh, my head! I feel like an elephant's been sleeping on me… George! George, wake up!

GEORGE: (Snorts and mumbles) Huh? Marcie, not again, I got to save it for my client, honey…

PAUL: George, Georgie—wake up!

GEORGE: (Snorts and wakes) What? Paul? What're you doing in my bed? What a nightmare, huh? I dreamed that Marcie had remodeled the bedroom as an animal graveyard.

PAUL: Wake up and smell the droppings, George. (George yawns) We're in an abandoned pet cemetery. We came here, remember, to pay off the Bow-Wowists…

GEORGE: Oh, yeah.

PAUL: …and get my wife back. Somehow they saw through your Ted Turner disguise.

GEORGE: Oh, that's right. They, they ripped off my moustache, and they—they shot us with something.

PAUL: Yeah, elephant tranquilizer.

GEORGE: Oh, how can I forget?

PAUL: They've got my 20 million dollars—and my wife!

GEORGE: Wait a minute, maybe not. Remember we—we heard her calling us from that rhinoceros crypt!

PAUL: Oh, yeah! Hey, gimme a hand, will ya?

SFX: EFFORTS

GEORGE: Here we go! (efforts) Up! Oh!

SFX: BANGING ON METAL DOOR

PAUL: Astrid? Astrid? Are you still in there?

ASTRID: (ON ECHO) Paul, Paul—I'm all right, honey. Just do what they say…

GEORGE: She sounds drugged.

PAUL: That's Astrid… Here, help we with these doors (efforts) Push! C'mon push! (efforts) They—they won't budge! Hey, c'mon, George help me, would ya?

GEORGE: Paul? Paul?

PAUL: What? C'mon! (more efforts)

GEORGE: Stop for a minute, will ya?

PAUL: What!?

GEORGE: They open OUT…

PAUL: Oh, oh, oh—yeah…

SFX: SQUEAKY DOORS OPEN

GEORGE: Can—can ya see anything?

PAUL: It's dark in here. Astrid?

ASTRID: (on echo) Paul, Paul—I'm all right, honey.

GEORGE: She's over there!

ASTRID: (on echo) Just do what they say…

PAUL: Ok, ok—listen—I'm coming, honey…

SFX: PAUL STUMBLES

PAUL: Ow! Ooooh…

ASTRID: (on echo) Paul, Paul—I'm all right, (runs down) honeeeeyyy…

GEORGE: Paul! She's dying!

PAUL: She's just… run down, George, look!

GEORGE: A voice-activated tape recorder!

PAUL: Sitting on something… Hey, c'mon, still got the flashlight?

GEORGE: Oh, yeah, yeah…

PAUL: Give it to me!

GEORGE: Here, here…

PAUL: Ohhhh!

GEORGE: Paul? Paul, what's wrong?

PAUL: This is a case of "Dead Wife Dog Food."

GEORGE: What!?

PAUL: Look at the label on one of these cans—

GEORGE: Give it to me, give it! (reading) "A full pound of ground round house spouse—in every can?" Oh, Paul. I'm so sorry…

PAUL: Ohhhh… ASTRIDDDD!!!!!

MFX: MUSIC STING

POWER #15: POW/E.R.

SFX: HOLISTIC CLINIC AMBIANCE

PAUL: (Waking) Ohhh, Astrid! Its so ironic. You were never
              any good in the kitchen. The only thing you ever fixed
              me came out of a can and—and now, now you're in a
              can… (Sobs hysterically)

DR. THORPE: Now, now, Mr. Power, stop torturing yourself.

DR. KLINE: That's *our* job. (laughs)

DR. THORPE: Please, Doctor Kline! You must forgive my colleague,
              Mr. Power—that's a joke from the dark ages of shock
              therapy!

PAUL: Huh? Eh—who are you people, and where am I?

DR. THORPE: Why, you're at the Kline/Thorpe Clinic at Ojai Hot
              Crystal Springs.

PAUL: What happened to my clothes?

DR. KLINE: They're being analyzed by our psychometric team for
              traces of past-life trauma.

PAUL: What are you talking about?

DR. THORPE: Don't worry about a thing; your friends, Mr. Scoff
              and Ms. Femme are taking care of everything.

DR. KLINE: Your task is simply—to be, to hear and to focus your
              mind, until you become as pure and pointed as the
              crystal stalactite you're sitting on.

PAUL: Oh, oh—is *that* what this is.

DR. THORPE: Yes, Paul. You are experiencing the purifying vibrations of the Kline/Thorpe High Colonic Crystal Throne!

PAUL   Get me off this thing, you quacks, so I can shove it up your a—

DR. THORPE: Paul—Paul—you're understandably enraged.

PAUL: Hey, it isn't every day that a man finds his wife ground up into pooch *pâté*.

DR. KLINE: Ohhhh…

DR. THORPE: Doctor Kline!

DR. KLINE: Doctor Thorpe! You know I advocate the school of Direct Traumatic Challenge.

DR. THORPE: Oh, yes! An approach that has already resulted in the destruction of three of our most promising patients.

DR. KLINE: Says you!

DR. THORPE: While I continue to champion the indirect approach of Holistic Self-Rationalization.

DR. KLINE: Wimp therapy!

DR. THORPE: Cassandra, look at us! (chuckles) We're mincing words while this poor man's wife has been reduced to mincemeat! Let's evince some adult behavior. Fix me a drink, sweetheart.

DR. KLINE: Fix your own drink, Otis.

DR. THORPE: All right, I will! (goes off)

DR. KLINE: Mr. Powers, can I call you Paul?

PAUL: No!

DR. KLINE: Okay. Actually, Paul, we're not sure if it is your wife in those cans. We opened one up, and frankly, those innards could belong to anyone; and the fact that the dogs liked it doesn't mean anything either. We all know that dogs have never been known for discriminating taste.

DR. THORPE: (coming on) You said it! What's a Matisse to a mutt? Have a martini, Paul.

PAUL: Thanks. (Sips) Ah, that's more like it.

DR. THORPE: And now, Paul—a toast—to all of us here, at the Kline/Thorpe Clinic in Ojai Crystal Hot Springs. May the power of the potion in these clear crystal goblets bring health and prosperity to the souls in this chamber—and wreck havoc and holocaust upon the heads of all Freudians, Jungians, Rogerians and that twisted troll, Dr. Ruth!

SFX: THEY DRINK

PAUL: I feel better already.

SFX: THEY SMASH THEIR GOBLETS

PAUL: What's next?

DR. THORPE: Ah! The hot tub. Don't get up…

PAUL: Well—ah, I can't.

DR. THORPE: I'll, I'll just wheel you in.

SFX: WHEELCHAIR EFFECT

PAUL: Oh-oh…

DR. THORPE: The waters are truly miraculous, Paul. They are
                     heated by the natural volcanic conditions of the
                     earth's crust, augmented by the activity of the nearby
                     underground nuclear test site! And here we are.

SFX: BUBBLING WATERS, WIND CHIMES

PAUL: (coughs) It's so steamy in here, I can hardly breathe…

DR. THORPE: It's time to eject—"yippee ki yooooooo!"

SFX: CHAIR BOINGS

PAUL: Ahhhhhhh…

POWER #16 SPLASH OF THE TITANS

SFX: BIG SPLASH, BUBBLING UNDER

ALEX: I give that an 8.2, Paul.

PAUL: (Sputtering and coughing) Alex! What're you doing here?

ALEX: I thought after a session with Dr. Kline and Dr. Thorpe, that a nice wet martini would be just the thing.

PAUL: Well, I'm ready for another.

ALEX: Just dip your glass. The whole hot tub is one big martini. Ooooh, (chuckles) there goes an olive.

PAUL: (laughs) Well after sitting on a 6-inch crystal with those New Age quacks for half an hour, I'm not sure what I need. By the way—how did I get here? I can't remember a thing after finding my wife ground up into dog food.

ALEX: Yes, George said you went over the edge, and I know this is a good place for bringing people back.

PAUL: You've—been here before?

ALEX: Why, sure. When you dumped me for Astrid, I came here to soak and dry out. Have another martini.

PAUL: No, I've gotta get back to the city.

ALEX: No, you don't. George is taking care of everything.

PAUL: He can't get my clients back, and he can't get my 20-million dollars back—uh—*your* 20-million dollars, Alex. It went down the elephant hole with those Bow-Wowists…

ALEX: Oh, I'm not worried.

PAUL: Oh, Alex, I love the fact that you have such faith in me.

ALEX: Well, yes, that too, Paul. But I'm not worried because I have your agency as collateral.

PAUL: Some collateral. I was counting on the good publicity from saving Astrid to win my clients back.

ALEX: You just take it easy, Paul. You're not doing anybody any good—

PAUL: I never did, and it made me a wealthy man.

ALEX: Well, you're in hot water now. So just relax and enjoy it.

SFX: DOOR OPENS

ALEX: Yes?

ROCKY: Ms. Femme, Ocean is ready to massage you now.

ALEX: Coming, Rocky. You just lie back and relax and have some lovely thoughts. Why don't you pretend you're just an innocent anchovy inside a little olive, bobbing around in the big martini of life…?

PAUL: "Innocent anchovy." That's nice copy, Alex.

ALEX: Thanks.

SFX: DOOR EFFECT

ALEX: Lock the door, Rocky.

ROCKY: Yes, Ma'am.

ALEX: Make sure Mr. Power is not disturbed until I return.

ROCKY: Very good, Ms. Femme, but remember, when used as directed, an alcohol bath can be dangerous to your health.

ALEX: Not to *my* health, I can assure you. As for Mr. Power—a good soaking is exactly what he needs.

ROCKY: Anything you say, Miss…

SFX: DOOR OPENS

MFX: EERIE TRANSITIONAL CHORD

POWER #17: GIN AND BENWAY

MFX: SUSPENSE STING UNDER

SFX: SIREN RUNS DOWN

PICO:	Give me a hand. (efforts)Ahhh, woof! Boy, what have we got here, man, a human cocktail? Whew…
ALV:	*Pero no*, Pico. This chico's more like a pickled prune.
PICO:	You're right, Alvarado. I think I seen him in Dick Tracy, no?
ALV:	Hey, *posiblemente*, man. Oh, oh, his hearing aid just fell out.
PICO:	Hey, no, man, that's an olive, man.
ALV:	Oh, wow, and look what they pumped out of his stomach.
PICO:	Let me see that, there. Ooh! *Dios Mio*, this tastes terrible. Needs an olive.
ALV:	Here!
PICO:	(slurps) That's better. Here try some.
ALV:	Yeah, yeah!

SFX: EMERGENCY ROOM AMBIANCE

ROSE:	Bring him in here, boys.

PICO: He's all yours, Doc. (Hic!)

PICO AND ALVARADO EXIT LAUGHING

ROSE: Dr. Benway, connect him up to life support. Glucose
             IV, slow drip. Well, how does the screen look?

BENWAY: Not too good. It's dropping fast.

ROSE: EKG?

BENWAY: No, no, IBM. I know I should have dumped it this
             morning. Where's my broker's number?

ROSE: Dr. Benway, get off the Financial Channel and put up
             his vital signs.

BENWAY: Oh, he's okay, Dr. Rose. Here's your "General Hospital".

SFX: SLOW BEEP OF AN EKG

ROSE: This man's barely with us. Give me his hemoglobin
             sample.

BENWAY: Here it is, Doctor.

ROSE: Ugh, looks more like a Bloody Mary.

BENWAY: A little light on the Tabasco, don't you think?

ROSE: This is the worse case of alcohol poisoning I've ever
             seen.

BENWAY: This guy, ah, what's his name? (READING) Paul
             Power? He's some, ah, party animal, huh? Hey, listen,
             Rosie, I've got a great idea. Why don't we just suck
             off a couple of liters of this guy's blood, go down to
             pathology and get stiff.

SFX: HOSPITAL ANNOUNCEMENTS IN BG

ROSE: Dr. Benway, pump him out again, stat, and then get
            him over to the dry wing at Ford Fairlane.

BENWAY: Okay, okay!

MFX: UPBEAT TECHO TRANSITION

POWER #18: MOONWALKER

MFX: TECHNO TRACK FADES OUT

SFX: HOSPITAL INTERCOM IN BG

MJ: Excuse, me, nurse?

NURSE: (Filipino accent) Ah! You're Michael Jackson!

MJ: Isn't Paul Power on this floor?

NURSE: Why, yes, Mr. Jackson, he right in there.

MJ: Oh, thank you.

NURSE: But his doctor is very particular about no visitors.

MJ: Oh, don't worry, he used to represent me.

NURSE: I'm very sorry, but—

MJ: I don't suppose an autograph would change your mind?

NURSE: Mmm, well…

MJ: This glove goes with it…

NURSE I really don't think that—

MJ: And a lock of my—ouch—hair?

NURSE: Oh, my!

MJ: And the epaulets off my jacket —

NURSE: Oh!

MJ: And—oh—something very, very special.

NURSE: What's that?

MJ: Hold out your hand…

SFX: HANDS HER SOMETHING

NURSE: Ooooh!

MJ: That's the Jackson Family Stamp—

NURSE: Oh…

MJ: You can get backstage anywhere with that!

NURSE: (squeals) He right in there!

MJ: Thank you.

SFX: DOOR OPENS, MONITORING DEVICE UNDER

PAUL: (snores and mumbles)

MJ: Paul? Paul? It's me, Michael.

PAUL: (Waking) Wha—what? Mi—Mi—Michael?

MJ: Yes.

PAUL: Michael! Don't leave me! Please, don't leave me.

MJ: Don't worry, Paul, I already have.

PAUL: Huh!?

MJ: But I'm coming back.

PAUL: You are?

MJ: Everybody's coming back to the agency.

PAUL: Oh, that's—that's marvelous, Michael! It's wonderful to have Hollywood at my feet again.

MJ: It's a whole new ballgame over there with Alex Femme at the helm.

PAUL: You're mixing your metaphors, Michael. Wait a minute, wait a minute, wait a—Alex Femme at the helm?

MJ: Uh-huh.

PAUL: Oh, that's right, she's just babysitting things for me.

MJ: And the baby's doing fine. Oh, it's too bad you missed the big party last night.

PAUL: What party?

MJ: Well, the reopening of the agency.

PAUL: Huh?

MJ: You'll love the new sign—"Femme-Power"? You can see it flashing all over Beverly Hills. Well, I gotta go, I'm due in the operating room.

PAUL: Oh, yeah? Well, what's wrong?

MJ: Oh, not a thing, just having my re-do finished. You like it?

PAUL: Well, from one angle, you look like your old voodoo-doll self, Mike, but—

MJ: And here—see?

PAUL: From the other angle, you look like Madonna!

MJ: Yeah! "Two (claps) two (claps) two stars in one!"
I come in with the glove, I'm the Michael you love—
I show the other condition, I'm Blonde Ambition!
So long...

PAUL: Nurse, nurse?

NURSE: Goo'bye, Mr. Jackson!

PAUL: Nurse!

NURSE: Wha' is it, Mr. Power?

PAUL: What day is this?

NURSE: T'ursday.

PAUL: Thursday, hmmm? The sixteenth?

NURSE: No, the t'enty t'ird.

PAUL: The *t'enty turd*? Oh, no, I've been here a week!

NURSE: Yes?

PAUL: I defaulted on the 20 million!

SFX: THE BEEPS ACCELERATE

PAUL: Alex owns my company! I gotta, I gotta stop her—

NURSE: Mr. Power...

PAUL: I gotta get outta here!

NURSE: Now, we're not going anywhere, Mr. Power. Lieutenant Weejan of the Bel Air police is due here any minute to question you about your addempted-a-suicide.

PAUL: My "addemted-a-suicide!?" Let me tell you something, nurse Papool, if I ever got to the point where I addemted-a-suicide, I'd kill myself first!

NURSE: All right, Mr. Power, let's not get ourselves up-a-set.

PAUL I am "up-a-set!"

NURSE: It's time for our little feel-good needle...

MFX: TECHO CYMBAL CRASH

POWER # 19: BEVERLY HILLS STREET BLUES

SFX: STREET AMBIANCE

WEEJUN: Hey, you!

GEORGE: What…what?

WEEJUN: Are you George Scoff?

GEORGE: Yes.

WEEJUN: I'm Lieutenant Weejun, Bel-Air Police.

GEORGE: So?

WEEJUN: Ah, you were acquainted with Paul Power, huh, the human highball lying in there?

GEORGE: Yeah, we're best friends. Lieutenant.

WEEJUN: Aha, then maybe you can tell me why your best friend tried to take his life.

GEORGE: Now, just a second.

WEEJUN: I don't have a second.

GEORGE: It was clearly an accident. He was overcome by a combination of heat and alcohol fumes.

WEEJUN: Sure.

GEORGE: And if it hadn't been for Ms. Femme, he would be dead.

WEEJUN: Dead, sooner or later, yeah, and probably sooner. Look what we found in the trunk of his car.

SFX: BOX DROPPED

GEORGE: Bunch of jars and tubes.

WEEJUN: Oh, yeah?

GEORGE: Well, maybe he's into making his own beer.

WEEJUN: This is a bier they'd carry him to his grave in. This is a suicide machine, buddy.

GEORGE: Oh, oh, I can explain that, Lieutenant.

WEEJUN: Well, I'm waiting.

GEORGE: Paul saw this as a way out of his financial difficulties.

WEEJUN: Exactly.

GEORGE: Now, come on, Lieutenant; Paul Power has everything to live for.

WEEJUN: Such as?

GEORGE: A wife…a business…a reputation… (WEEJUN LAUGHS) Maybe you're right.

WEEJUN: Ex-actly.

GEORGE: Stop saying that! Look, Lieutenant Weejun, I insist on being present during this interrogation. As I said, I am Paul's best friend…

WEEJUN: Yeah, you said that.

GEORGE: And I am also his lawyer, and If I allow him to play into the hands of the authorities, it will prejudice his abilities to pay my bill.

WEEJUN: They told me you were a crack lawyer.

GEORGE: Well, I used to be; but since it's moved to the ghetto, there's no money in it.

WEEJUN: You're telling me.

SFX: DOOR OPENS, SNORING IN B.G.

GEORGE: Oh, look, he's sleeping like a baby.

WEEJUN: Yeah, a pickled baby.

GEORGE: Shhh! Paul, Paul, why did you do it? I told you I was having that dog food analyzed, and if that was Astrid in that can, she ran eighth at Belmont last week. Paul, are you listening? Let me get the covers off your head.

SFX: COVERS PULLED BACK

WEEJUN: Hey!

NURSE: (moaning) Oh, oh.

GEORGE: Holy smoke, it's Nurse Papool, and…she's naked!

WEEJUN: Yeah, except for that needle in her arm. Now, don't touch a thing, Scoff.

GEORGE: Why not?

WEEJUN: I'm going to take some pictures. I'm gonna get a nice close up of that sweet Filipino…

SFX: POLAROIDS SNAPPED

POWER #20: POWER'S END

MFX: TECHNO WAH-WAH

SFX: STREET AMBIANCE UNDER

PAUL: Excuse me, Ma'am.

MOM: Yes—ah—nurse?

PAUL: Say, ah, could you lend me your telephone credit card?

DAD: Oh, gosh, look at her, honey—a homeless nurse. Hmmm, fell right through the safety net. What is this world coming to?

TIFF: Um, Daddy?

DAD: What, Tiff?

TIFF: Why does that nurse have hairy legs?

DAD: (chuckles) Tiffany! She's experiencing a temporary cash flow crisis, honey, and at this point in time, she just doesn't have the disposable income for depilatories.

TIFF: Oh, you mean God doesn't love her.

MOM: Tiffany? (Dad chuckles) What have they been teaching you at Miss Imelda's? Here, give the poor lady this, so she can make her call.

TIFF: Here, poor lady.

PAUL: What's this, kid?

TIFF: It's a quarter.

PAUL: A quarter o' what?

MOM: A quarter of a dollar, my dear.

PAUL: Yeah? What's "a dollar"? Hey, hey—is that anything like a hundred?

DAD: Here, here—let us help you, ma'am. Just put it in here.

SFX: COIN IN PAYPHONE

PAUL: Oh, that's where it goes, huh?

MOM: Now, what's the number?

PAUL: "I-M, P-O-W-E-R."

SFX: PUNCHING IN LETTERS

MOM: There ya go, nurse.

SFX: PHONE AMBIANCE, RINGS AND PICKS UP

MALE: (ON FILTER British accent) Femme Power.

PAUL: Paul Power.

MALE: I'm sorry, Mr. Power is no longer among us.

PAUL: I am Power!

MALE: That's our number. Whom do you wish to speak with?

PAUL: All right, give me Alex.

MALE: All right, which one?

PAUL: Huh?

MALE: As of yesterday, everybody here is named Alex.

PAUL: Well, give me Alex Femme, the heartless shark.

MALE: Oh, Alex One! Whom shall I say is calling?

PAUL: Hmm—tell her it's Sadam Hussein.

MALE: Oh! Oh! She's been expecting your call, Your—Your Thingness. I'll put you right through.

ALEX: (on filter) *Mahabar, Sadam*! I've got great news. I have Golem Globus on the other line. It's a GO for the invasion mini-series. Now listen to the working title: "Iraq-na-phobia"! Don't you love it?

PAUL: Alex, it's Paul.

ALEX: Paul, how nice to hear from you. How are things at the dry out wing at Ford Fairlane?

PAUL: I wouldn't know.

ALEX: Oh, are you feeling better after your little accident?

PAUL: I'm beginning to feel it was no accident, Alex.

ALEX: Then you're getting better.

PAUL: Alex, we've got to have a talk. I'm deeply concerned about your taking over my business.

ALEX: Don't you trust me?

PAUL   Absolutely. Not!

ALEX: Hmm, you really are getting better. I could come out and visit you. Let's see, uh, is the end of next week good for you?

PAUL: I'm no longer in the hospital.

ALEX: Oh, really, Paul? Where are you?

PAUL: Well, that's for me to know and you to find out.

ALEX: I can do that.

SFX: PHONE BEEP

ALEX: Oh! You're at a payphone on Skid Drive in Beverly Hills.

PAUL: Yes, Alex, and I'm wearing a nurse's uniform.

ALEX: Oh, (Giggles) I like that.

PAUL: You would.

ALEX: Just a minute, Paul.

SFX: CALL INTERRUPTION

ALEX: Yes, Alex Twelve?

PAUL: Alex…

ALEX: Paul, I've got the REAL Saddam Hussein on the line. Hold for a minute.

PAUL: What?

MFX: HOLD MUSIC ON FILTER

PAUL: I hate Muzak. I hate being on hold!

MALE:	(on filter) Mr. Power?
PAUL:	Yeah?
MALE:	Sandy—I mean, Alex Twelve, here, and Ms. Femme told me to tell you that you may be on hold for 7 hours.
PAUL:	What?
MALE:	Are there any particular sections of the Boston Pops you'd like to hear? They use real cannons, you know, in the 1812 Overture.
PAUL:	Put me on the old hold-forever routine, eh? I know that one, I invented it! Ha ha ha ha, they think I'm finished—but I'll be back—bigger and better and stronger and meaner than ever!

SFX: OUTDOOR TRAFFIC AMBIANCE UNDER

GUY:	Yeah, yeah, you tell 'em, nursie, yeah, I love it. Sounds like me, six months ago. They said I was finished, but look at me now, huh?
PAUL:	Do I have to?
GUY:	Yeah, right, I'm a bum, I'm a bum, huh? Do you recognize me without the beard, without the pants?
PAUL:	Will you get out of my way?
GUY:	Now, listen, listen, listen to me. I used to be on the front page of the Wall Street Journal every day; now I sleep under it every night. Look, look, look—can you still make out the monogram on my shirt?
PAUL:	(reading) B—Dollar Sign...

GUY: "BS, BS, BS, BS!" Which stands for—huh?—Bernie—huh? Silver? Bernie Silver—Bernie Silver?

PAUL: Get on with it.

GUY: Bernie Silverado!

PAUL: Bernie Silverado!

GUY: Bernie Silverado!

PAUL: Wait a minute, you took the fall for the President's son in the S&L scam!

GUY: Ahhhh, S&L: "Snakes and Lepers," that's the way they treat us now!

PAUL: You mean there's—ah—more of you down here on Skid Drive?

GUY: Just wait, just wait—yeah—just wait until the free cheese giveaway tonight at the back of Le Bistro. There's so much top management on the bottom now, we call ourselves "The Unfortunate 500."

PAUL: Bernie, that gives me an idea…

GUY: Yeah, me, too, cutie. How about a date, huh? What're ya doing for dinner? We could do a coupla dumpsters together, huh?

PAUL: Bernie, look—

GUY: I'm lookin'!

SFX: RIPPING OFF OF CLOTHES

PAUL: I'm a man! I spell M-A-N.

GUY: Aw, jeez, I don't know diddly! I thought you were
            Mediterranean, huh? What's your name?

PAUL: Paul—uh—Midas.

GUY: Midas.

PAUL: *Max* Midas. Everyone I touch turns to gold.

GUY: Oh, yeah? Excuse me for asking, "Max", but, ah,
            what are you doing down here on Skid Drive—in a
            skirt?

PAUL: Head hunting, Bernie.

GUY: Yeah?

PAUL: I'm looking for hungry, ruthless, amoral, frustrated,
            ruined professionals.

GUY: Yeah, like me, huh, like me?

PAUL: Yeah, like you, Bernie.

GUY: Well, you *would* like me. Here I am! What'd you
            have in mind? Bank fraud, money laundering, price
            fixing—uh—toxic waste recycling?

PAUL: Pieces of the puzzle, Bernie, just pieces of the puzzle.
            I've got something much bigger on the burner.

GUY: Yeah?

PAUL: How would you like to help me take over the world?

GUY: Ooooh—is there a dental plan?

MFX: SERIES END MUSIC UNDER

ANN: "Power!" Created by and starring Peter Bergman
and Philip Proctor. Co-starring Melinda Peterson
and featuring Patricia Stallone. Recorded by Jerry
Summers and Bob Carlson. Produced by Ted
Bonnitt, Executive Producer, Steve Rath. This is your
announcer, A. Ernest Guy. Proctor & Bergman's
"Power" was recorded at KCRW for National Public
Radio's "Heat with John Hockenberry," a production
of Murray Street Enterprise and KQED-FM, copyright
1990. "Power!"

Firesign Theatre at BearManor Media
www.beamanormedia.com

www.ingramcontent.com/pod-product-compliance
Lightning Source LLC
Chambersburg PA
CBHW050413030726
47503CB00006B/2172